This book
belongs to

.... Ella ....

For Jill and Manish, with love

FREDERICK WARNE

Published by the Penguin Group
Penguin Books Ltd, 80 Strand, London WC2R 0RL, England
Penguin Young Readers Group, 345 Hudson Street,
New York, New York 10014, U.S.A.
Penguin Books Australia Ltd, 250 Camberwell Road, Camberwell,
Victoria 3124, Australia
Canada, India, New Zealand, South Africa

1 3 5 7 9 10 8 6 4 2

ISBN-13: 978 07232 5886 5

Printed in Great Britain

Jasmine's Starry Night

by Kay Woodward

Welcome to the Flower Fairies' Garden!

Where are the fairies?
Where can we find them?
We've seen the fairy-rings
They leave behind them!

Is it a secret
No one is telling?
Why, in your garden
Surely they're dwelling!

No need for journeying,
Seeking afar:
Where there are flowers,
There fairies are!

Contents

Chapter One

Once Upon a Summer's Day

Snip, snippity-snip, *snip*!

'Perfect,' said Jasmine. She was finished at last. Stretching her gossamer wings, the dainty Flower Fairy floated down from the lofty stem where she was perched and landed silently on the ground below. Carefully, she lay down her fairy pruning shears – made from two tiny pieces of flint wrapped with a length of leafy twine – and stepped back to admire her handiwork.

'Oooh . . .' she breathed, sweeping dark-blonde curls from her eyes. It really did look wonderful. A great leafy arch of jasmine curved high above her head – vibrant green leaves studded with star-shaped flowers of dazzling white and softest pink. The hot, summer's sun twinkled like diamonds between chinks in the foliage.

Unlike other, wilder plants that flourished in and around the Flower Fairies' Garden, the jasmine plant was very

well behaved, preferring to climb steadily rather than run amok. The wooden trellis, constructed so long ago that none of the fairies could remember who had built it, was the ideal place for the plant to grow. And thanks to Jasmine's skilful shears, it was neat and tidy, with no straggling stems or wilting petals.

A big, fat bumblebee droned past, pausing to investigate an inviting white flower. 'Bzzz,' it hummed contentedly.

'Help yourself,' said Jasmine cheerily. She knew how delicious her pollen and nectar were to bees. She also knew that there was more than enough to satisfy a whole swarm *and* make a heap of precious fairy dust. But watching the bee made Jasmine realize how thirsty she was too and she soon began to long for a nutshell of Elderberry's delicious juice.

'If only Elderberry weren't so far away...' mused Jasmine as she sipped from a buttercup full of dew instead. 'And if only I knew her well enough to ask her for a drink.' She shrugged and settled herself in the leafy shade of her flowery bower.

One of these days, Jasmine vowed, she would overcome her shyness and meet some new Flower Fairies. But not right now. The scorching sun made things *so* uncomfortably hot ... and it was *so* difficult to think of

interesting things to say . . . and it would be *so* much easier just to snooze the afternoon away in the shade of her flower until dusk fell. Maybe *then* she would feel braver . . . With a sleepy sigh, she lay back against a cool leaf and drifted off into a wonderful daydream in which crowds of Flower Fairy friends flocked round, each eager to listen to Jasmine's views on the very latest happenings in their beautiful garden –

'Oy!'

Jasmine's eyes sprang open. She looked in bewilderment at the face framed with unruly chestnut hair that loomed above her. The Flower Fairy was clad in yellow and green, with *the* most magnificent yellow and black wings sprouting from his shoulders. Who *was* he?

'I say,' said the mysterious visitor, his dark eyes sparkling with mischief. 'You can sleep

for Flower Fairyland, can't you? I've been
trying to wake you for ages!' He grasped
Jasmine's hand firmly and pumped it up and
down. 'I'm Dandelion,' he announced. 'And
you are ... ?'

'Jasmine,' she replied timidly, unused to
such boisterous behaviour. She hurried to
her feet, running her fingers over her pinky-
white silken dress to smooth out the creases.

'Pleased to meet you, Jasmine,' said
Dandelion, his eyes straying to the starry

flowers that surrounded them. 'Nice petals you have here. Lovely flowers. Are these the ones that smell wonderful at night?'

Jasmine nodded wordlessly as Dandelion surged on.

'I'm not from around these parts, myself,' he explained. 'Just passing through, seeing the sights, meeting new Flower Fairies. You know how it is.'

She nodded again, even though she had no idea how it was, never having ventured further than the garden wall. There didn't seem any point in travelling far, not when the thing she loved to do most was relax right here – among the fragrant petals of her own flower – and watch the wonderful, twinkling stars that filled the night sky. According to Flower Fairy folklore, stars were really pinpricks in the dark covering of night, and light shone through these tiny holes to make starlight.

'So what do you have planned for such
a fine summer's day?' asked Dandelion,
pausing for breath at last. He raised an
inquisitive eyebrow.

'I . . . er . . . well, er . . .' All at once, Jasmine
wanted so badly to impress this globetrotting
fairy, but the truth was, she'd been planning
on sleeping. She'd stayed up incredibly late
last night, watching the dazzling display of

shooting stars that had lit up the sky with their magic. And now she was *very* tired.

'There's no need to look so worried,' said Dandelion kindly. 'I only ask because I was thinking of taking a stroll around the Flower Fairies' garden. I'd be delighted if you'd accompany me for a spot of sightseeing.' He winked. 'What do you say? I bet you'd be an excellent tour guide.'

Dandelion's good humour was infectious and despite her plans for a lazy afternoon, Jasmine found herself agreeing. 'OK,' she said shyly. 'Some of the older Flower Fairies have travelled to the Fairy Fair today as it's a full moon tonight, but the younger ones are still around. Shall we visit Rose? She has the most fantastic garden.'

'You're the boss!' said Dandelion. He delved into his backpack and produced a bright yellow dandelion. 'My parasol!' he

said proudly, holding it high above their
heads to shade them from the sun. He looped
his other hand through Jasmine's arm and
together they set off around the garden.

It was a wonderful afternoon. Dandelion
was so thrilled with Rose's glamorous
flowers – and the dark, secret tunnel they
had to creep along to reach the rose garden
itself – that Jasmine became more and more

confident with her suggestions. Before long, they'd also visited Pansy, who was teaching the younger Flower Fairies to dance, admired Sycamore's treetop gymnastics and sampled a handful of Candytuft's freshly made fudge.

'Mmm . . . delicious,' said Dandelion, licking his lips. He leant back against the towering oak tree and admired the view. 'This place is so full of energy!' he announced, wide-eyed, and turned to Jasmine. 'What a wonderful place to live . . . there are a million and one things going on!'

Jasmine smiled, feeling incredibly proud of her Flower Fairy friends. They certainly were a busy lot. If they weren't tending to their flowers, they were making fairy dust. And if they weren't making fairy dust, then they might be doing anything from learning to speak Bumblebee – a difficult language that involved countless ways of pronouncing *bzzz* – to skipping with Sweet Pea's long twirly stems.

'So what about you?' asked Dandelion.

'Huh?' said Jasmine, quickly remembering her manners. 'I mean . . . pardon?'

'What do you do in your spare time?' he said. 'What's *your* hobby?'

Lost for words, Jasmine stared at him as, slowly, the most dreadful thought occurred to her. She didn't *have* a hobby. She did *nothing* in her spare time. Whatever would Dandelion think of her now? Would he vanish quicker than hailstones in the sunshine?

Flower Fairies are the politest, most kind-hearted creatures in the world. When Jasmine revealed her embarrassing secret to Dandelion, he didn't fly away or laugh scornfully or do any of the other horrid things she'd imagined. Instead, he gently patted her shoulder and told her that she simply hadn't found the right hobby yet.

'But what if I *don't*?' wailed Jasmine. 'What if I *never* find it?'

'You will,' said Dandelion, with a knowing nod. 'Everyone has something that they like to do to relax. It's just a

case of finding out what that something is. And you might already be doing it – your hobby could be taking care of your beautiful flower!'

'Oh . . .' said Jasmine. She hadn't thought of that. But as dusk fell and she returned home, clambering up to the very top of her wooden trellis, which was by far the best place to see the stars, doubts began to grow in her mind. All of the other Flower Fairies found time to look after their flower *and* do their own thing . . .

For example, Lavender liked nothing better than to wash the other Flower Fairies' clothes. And however much she wanted her own hobby, Jasmine couldn't see herself doing this – where was the fun in soapsuds?

Candytuft searched the length and breadth of Flower Fairyland to find yummy ingredients for her legendary sweets. Now,

Jasmine loved to *taste* Candytuft's treats, but she knew from experience that she wasn't cut out for cookery.

And what about Sycamore? Only last week he'd perfected the triple somersault, after weeks of high-flying practice. Jasmine simply wasn't this adventurous.

She sighed.
How could she *ever* hope to
come up with an idea that was
anywhere near as practical *or* tasty
or exciting as the other Flower Fairies'
hobbies? Her eyes glistened with sparkling
tears ... but before they had a chance to
tumble down her cheeks, Jasmine felt a
feathery touch on her brow.

'Dear moth ...' she whispered, very quietly
so that she didn't frighten the shy creature
away. 'How lovely to see you. Have you
come far?'

The moth made
a soft rustling noise
in reply and landed
briefly on a gleaming
blossom, before
launching into the air
and hovering there.

Its beautiful wings glowed in the silvery moonlight. Jasmine saw that they were decorated with a black and white pattern so delicate that it might have been drawn by a fairy quill pen.

Whoosh! Without warning, the moth flew across the sky – and was gone.

'Well, what was all that about?' murmured Jasmine, wishing that she could have

understood the mysterious rustling noise. (Unfortunately, Moth was an even more difficult language than Bumblebee and she hadn't got the hang of it yet.) She shrugged and went back to thinking of a truly splendid hobby for herself.

Ballet dancing? No, she wasn't bendy enough.

Singing? No good either – she would feel too shy to sing in front of anyone else.

'It's no good,' she groaned. 'I'll *never* be able to find a hobby which is as interesting as the other Flower Fairies.'

'Ooooh . . .'

'Wow!'

'Did you *see* that?'

All thoughts of hobbies whizzed away as Jasmine suddenly became aware of the strangest sounds floating across the Flower Fairies' Garden.

'*So* cool!'

The whispers were loud – far too loud to belong to a tiny fairy. This could mean only one thing . . .

There were *children* in the Flower Fairies' Garden!

Chapter Three
Stargazing

Jasmine had heard rumours that children were kind creatures, but they were so big and *so* nosy. When she was younger, Jasmine had listened with awe to the stories of boys and girls searching for Flower Fairies at the bottom of the garden, which is where they seemed to think all fairies lived. The Flower Fairies chuckled at this. If only children knew that fairies could be found *anywhere* in the garden – sitting on a twig, hidden inside a flower or under a fallen leaf!

'Aaaa–mazing!'

The loud whisper reminded Jasmine of the seriousness of

the situation. The Flower Fairy Law – which stated that fairies should stay out of sight of people at all times – had been introduced by Kingcup and Queen of the Meadow to protect the Flower Fairies. Humans must *never* be allowed to see fairies. For if they knew that Flower Fairies existed, the tiny creatures would never be left alone.

Gathering her courage – and a handful of fairy dust in case of an emergency – Jasmine leapt from her petal perch, jumping nimbly from stem to stem until she reached the ground. Her mind was made up. It was very late – well past bedtime – so she figured that something strange *must* be afoot. Staying well out of sight, she would approach the children and find out exactly what they were up to.

'This is an *excellent* plan,' Jasmine whispered to herself, wondering absent-mindedly if hide-and-seek qualified as a proper hobby. On the quietest of tiptoes, she set off across the garden. It was chilly now

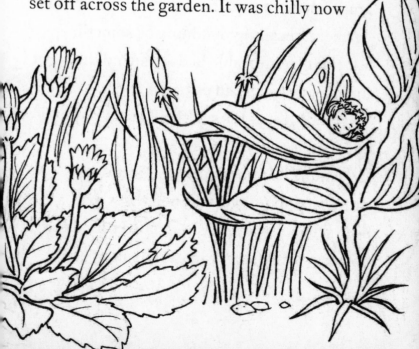

that the sun had gone down, so she gathered her flimsy frock tightly around her. Here and there she spotted a Flower Fairy, snugly warm under a blossomy quilt, and longed for the warmth and safety of her own flower. But she crept onwards.

Soon, a peculiar shape loomed up before her – a huge yellowy-green dome that seemed to glow in the moonlight. Now Jasmine was the one who felt like *ooohing* in amazement. She realized that this thing must be a tent, recalling that humans sometimes left their comfortable beds to spend the night under canvas instead of under roofs. 'Shreya, Milly – look at this!' said a boy's voice.

Jasmine leapt back into the shadow of a towering foxglove, terrified that she'd been seen. Nervously, she peeped round the flower's sturdy stem and caught sight of a small, dark-haired boy sitting in the tent's opening. He was clutching a circular chart in one hand and a torch in the other. His eyes were fixed firmly on the chart. Sitting on one side was a girl so like him that they must be

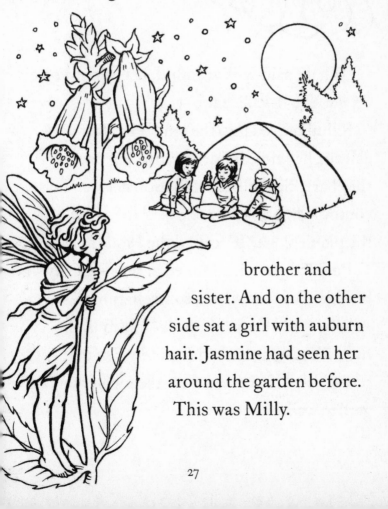

brother and sister. And on the other side sat a girl with auburn hair. Jasmine had seen her around the garden before. This was Milly.

'What?' said Milly. 'Rahul, keep your voice down. You'll wake Sam.'

Rahul peered into the tent. 'He's fast asleep,' he said confidently, turning back to the chart. 'See this constellation here . . .' he continued. 'Look, the one near the middle of the planisphere? It's called the Plough.'

Puzzled, Jasmine looked at the night sky. She hadn't a clue what a constellation was. All she could see were stars – millions of them. And none looked remotely like the plough she'd once seen from the top of the garden wall.

'Great,' said Shreya, yawning. '*Now* can we go to sleep?'

'Absolutely not,' said Rahul. 'If you close your eyes, you'll miss all of this!' He gestured at the twinkling sky. 'Tell you what . . . If you'll allow me to dazzle and amaze you with star facts, I'll let you go to sleep. Deal?'

Shreya and Milly giggled. 'Deal,' they said.

Rahul grinned. 'If Mum had let me bring my telescope over here, we'd be able to see the starry sky even better . . . But she said it was much too big and awkward to take camping and that there'd be no room for us to sleep.' He chuckled. 'I bet she wishes I didn't have such a complicated hobby!'

Jasmine shrank back into the shadows. A hobby . . . ? She could hardly believe her ears. She'd been worrying so much about finding her very own hobby and now it seemed that she'd had one all along. Even if she didn't have a clue what constellations, charts and telescopes were, it seemed that stargazing itself was a popular pastime! She performed a celebratory jig on the damp grass, much to the amusement of a nearby owl. Then she wrapped a fallen petal around her shoulders and settled down to listen, eagerly soaking

up Rahul's whispered words.

Sometime later, Jasmine was still gazing at the sky. She was stunned by what she'd learnt. Stars weren't pinpricks in the covering of night ... they were even more wonderful! The little Flower Fairy was awestruck now that she knew what it was all about.

'Wow,' said Shreya softly. 'What a beautiful star ...'

Rahul gave a low, admiring whistle. 'That's no star,' he said. 'That's a comet.'

Oblivious to danger, Jasmine wandered into the open, gazing curiously at the heavens. She saw it immediately. Where yesterday there had been nothing, there was now a shining star with its own tail, just visible against the inky darkness. And it was moving v-e-r-y s-l-o-w-l-y through the night sky. In some ways, it reminded her of the graceful moth.

Jasmine breathed in sharply. Had the

moth been trying
to let her know of
the arrival of this
strange star – this
'comet'? How lovely!

'Zzzz . . .'

Hopping into the air with
fright, Jasmine looked all around for
the source of the strange noise. And then she
giggled with relief. Foxglove had shimmied
halfway up his flower's thick stem and fallen
fast asleep, holding on tight. He was snoring
lightly, his purple-slippered feet dangling in
the breeze.

'What was *that*?' said Shreya.

Jasmine froze.

'What was *what*?' asked Rahul, still
staring upwards. 'You mean something up
there?'

'No, down here on earth . . .' Shreya

whispered. 'Near the foxglove. I'm sure I saw something twinkle in the grass.'

'Do you think it might have been a fairy?' murmured Milly hopefully.

Inwardly, Jasmine scolded herself for her stupidity. She *knew* the Flower Fairy Law. She *knew* that she should stay out of sight. And *now* look what had happened! Slowly, oh so slowly, she moved her hand towards the secret pocket where she kept her fairy dust. Would she be able to distract the children in time?

Taking a hefty pinch of fairy dust, Jasmine tossed it upwards. *Whoosh!* As the tiny particles floated back down to earth, the air began to shimmer magically, hiding her from sight. The Flower Fairy took her chance – and ran.

'Wow!' said Rahul.

'What?' cried Shreya. 'Have you seen a real

fairy?'

Rahul tutted. 'No, silly. Shooting stars – look!'

All three children stared up at the sky and the shining stars that whizzed over their heads. They didn't see the tiny fairy fleeing out of sight.

Jasmine was safe.

Chapter Four
Panic in the Garden

If Jasmine had been competing in the Fairy Sports Day, she would have won the long distance race hands down. Her bare feet were a blur as she sprinted through the garden, with her frantically beating wings lifting her up, up, up into the air every few seconds to avoid low bushes.

The frightened fairy headed for the safety of her trellis. It was the perfect hiding place. Because her dainty frock was made from the pinkest of its petals, she could simply curl up and pretend to be a flower. But on the way, she became aware of a high-pitched noise – an awful sort of squawking squeal – that made her run even faster. What could it *be*?

Eeeeeeeeeeeooooooooeeeeeek!

Jasmine soon realized that the noise was coming from the nursery. Of course! It was bound to be very busy tonight. Forget-me-not – one of the kindest, most caring fairies in the garden – had offered to babysit all of the youngest Flower Fairies while the older ones went to the Fairy Fair. But why was there such a racket?

Quickly changing direction, Jasmine headed towards the nursery, skidding to a halt as she saw a mob of young Flower

Fairies stampeding towards her. Too late!
The frantic creatures crashed into her,
toppling Jasmine to the ground. 'Ouch!' she
said, struggling to sit up under the weight
of wriggling arms and legs. 'Er . . . what's
wrong?'

'It's awful!' cried Herb Robert, his pointy
ears twitching wildly. 'The s-s-stars won't
keep s-s-still. They keep whizzing about!'

'They're going to tumble out of the sky,
aren't they?' squeaked White Clover. She
scrambled to her feet, her usually pink

cheeks now puce. 'The stars will drop into
Flower Fairyland and smash into a million
pieces —'

'And we'll never have starlight again!'
wailed Heather. '*Eeeeeeoooooeeeeek!*'

Jasmine winced and quickly plugged her
ears, thinking that at least she'd solved the
mystery of the dreadful sound. Calming
everyone might be more difficult. 'There's
really no need to worry,' she began tentatively.

No one heard. This was hardly surprising.
Jasmine was such a shy fairy that she rarely
spoke louder than a whisper. And there was

an awful lot of noise to compete with.

'I'm getting d-d-dizzy,' said a trembling Herb Robert, who was mesmerized by the shooting stars. He stared up at the sky, gently swaying on the spot. 'Look at them go . . . Zing, zing, *zing*!'

'I don't *like* it!' bawled White Clover, rubbing her chubby fists in her eyes.

Jasmine tried again. 'If you'll just listen for a moment —'

This time, she was interrupted by Forget-me-not, who arrived in a flurry of fluttering, her beautiful wings and silken frock glowing pale blue in the moonlight. 'You *mustn't* run away from me,' said the

Flower Fairy crossly, her pretty face creased with worry. 'I'm supposed to be looking after you!'

'But the stars are f-f-falling out of the sky!' cried Herb Robert.

'*Eeeeeooooooeeeeek!*' wailed Heather.

If Jasmine didn't do something soon, the children would hear the commotion. Then they would investigate. And then the Flower Fairies would be discovered. Crowds of fairy-mad humans would be trampling all over their precious garden before they knew it.

Suddenly, Jasmine knew what she must

do. She took a deep breath. She looked up at the sky and in a voice that was sweeter than honey and softer than petals, she started to sing her favourite lullaby . . .

'Twinkle, twinkle, little star
How I wonder what you are!
Up above the world so high,
Like a diamond in the sky.

When the blazing sun is gone,
When he nothing shines upon,
Then you show your little light,
Twinkle, twinkle, all the night.

Twinkle, twinkle, little star
How I wonder what you are!'

After a few seconds, Jasmine realized something quite astonishing. There was

absolute silence. Herb Robert had stopped shouting, White Clover had stopped crying and – thank the starry heavens – Heather had stopped that dreadful wailing. All of the young Flower Fairies were now sitting cross-legged at her feet, utterly entranced by the melody. And what's more, even though she had an audience, Jasmine didn't feel in the slightest bit shy.

'Do it again,' whispered Herb Robert. 'Please?'

Jasmine smiled. 'Later,' she said to the eager fairy. 'First, we're going on a little journey . . .'

Chapter Five
A Night Full of Stars

With so many humans about, it really wasn't safe in the open. So Jasmine suggested to Forget-me-not that they shepherded all of the young Flower Fairies to her wooden trellis instead, which was much closer.

'There's bags of room for everyone to snuggle down,' Jasmine said. 'And there's a terrific view of the sky too. It really is the ideal spot for a bedtime story.'

Forget-me-not frowned. 'But is it safe?' she asked. 'There are hundreds of stars zooming about tonight – what if one *does* fall into our garden? Just

imagine the noise Heather would make then
… No, I think we should be under cover.'
She scratched her head. 'Zinnia has the
most amazing leaves – why don't we shelter
beneath those?'

But Jasmine was firm. 'Trust me,' she
said, suddenly filled with more confidence
than she'd ever had in her life. Could it be
true that she was the only Flower Fairy who
understood what was going on in the night

sky? Well, if so, it was up to her to explain all. 'Everything will be fine,' she said, putting a comforting arm around Forget-me-not's quivering shoulder. 'Come on … let's get moving. There really is nothing to be afraid of.'

At last, Forget-me-not agreed. With a great deal of shushing, the young fairies linked hands and crept across the Flower Fairies' Garden in a long, twisty crocodile.

In the stillness of the night, even the slightest noise seemed deafening. Tiny twigs cracked underfoot like thunderclaps. Each time a leaf rustled, it sounded as if a gale-force wind was hurtling through the garden. And it was *so* spooky. The moonlight cast such long, scary shadows . . . and when the wind blew the flowers, the plants and the trees, the shadows moved too.

Everyone was very jittery, little Herb Robert most of all. 'Arrrggggghhhh!' he howled suddenly. 'I stepped into a swamp! It's going to suck me under . . . *Help!*'

'It's OK,' said Jasmine in her calmest voice. She threw a smidgen of fairy dust into the air – at once, the air was filled with glowing sparkles of light. 'Look closer,' she said. 'It's not a swamp – it's a ripe berry. You squished it under your foot.'

'Oh,' said Herb Robert, biting his lip

nervously. 'Well, that's all right, then.'

Luckily, there wasn't much further to go.

'We're here!' called Jasmine, directing the Flower Fairies up the wooden trellis.

'Up you go,' she said. 'Right to the top!'

'Oooh, it smells so . . . so . . . lovely!' White Clover announced. 'And your flowers are still open, even though the sun has set. I *like* it here.' Grinning happily, she plumped herself down next to the nearest pinky-white blossom and sniffed deeply. 'Ahh . . .' she sighed

contentedly.

Soon, everyone had found themselves a comfortable spot among the glimmering flowers. Jasmine made her way to the very top of the arch. From here, she could see everyone, and everyone could see her. She gulped. 'Well, this is it . . .' she muttered under her breath. Aloud, she said, 'Ahem.'

At once, eager faces swivelled towards her, like sunflowers turning to face the sun.

'Welcome to the greatest show on earth,' she said. 'It is with the greatest pleasure that

I present . . . the starry sky!' She threw her arms wide.

There were one or two hesitant claps, but the majority of the Flower Fairies just looked confused and scared.

'Let me explain,' said Jasmine, smiling broadly as she warmed to her topic. Thanks to the children, she now knew so many wonderful things. 'Stars aren't scary or creepy or spooky,' she said. 'A star is just a faraway sun, that's all. And that sun shines down on other worlds, maybe even on other Flower Fairies.'

'Wow,' said Heather. 'Just . . . wow.'

'So what about the falling stars?' demanded White Clover. 'Are they suns too? Are they pinging about in outer space, just waiting to crash into Flower Fairyland?'

'I knew it!' cried Herb Robert, leaping into the air and making the trellis wobble alarmingly. 'Everybody, run! Hide! Save yourselves!'

'Shush!' said Heather, holding a stern finger to her lips. 'I want to listen.'

'Well,' continued Jasmine mysteriously, 'shooting stars are even *more* amazing. Would you believe that each one is really a harmless bit of space stuff, probably no bigger than a sprinkling of fairy dust?'

Clover wasn't convinced. 'Then why do they shine so brightly?' she asked

suspiciously. Her face brightened. 'It's because they're magic, isn't it?'

'Not at all,' replied Jasmine. 'But they're travelling so quickly through space that when they bump into the air around our planet, they burst into flames –'

'And *then* they smash into Flower Fairyland!' howled Herb Robert.

'No,' said Jasmine. 'They burn up – and then they vanish.'

'Oh,' said Herb Robert. And sat down.

Once they realized there was no danger of the Flower Fairies' Garden going up in smoke, the fairies relaxed. So Jasmine told them about the Northern Lights – great,

shimmering curtains of multicoloured light that were said to appear in the night sky. 'I've never seen them, but I hope to ... one day,' she said wistfully. Next, she told them about comets – how they were really balls of ice and rock that hurtled through space.

But the Flower Fairies wanted to know more – much more. Why did the moon change from a curly crescent to a big shining ball and back again? Why couldn't they see stars in the daytime? Why did stars twinkle if they weren't magic?

Jasmine replied to their questions as best she could, but eventually even *she* was struggling to keep up. 'Enough!' she pleaded. 'I'm exhausted – so you must be too.' It was true. Even though their cheeks glowed with excitement, it was clear that the young fairies were fighting to stay awake.

'I'm sure Jasmine would be more than

happy to tell you more about the stars
another night,' a voice chipped in.

'Oh, absolutely,' said Jasmine quickly.
'There's how to spot a planet, how to find
your way by following the stars and . . .' her
words petered out. 'Er . . . who *is* that?' she
asked curiously. The voice had been deep and
charming and strangely familiar. But it didn't
belong to any of the Flower Fairies who'd
gathered to hear her starry tales.

With a sparkling whoosh of fairy dust,
a tall, brightly dressed fairy leapt right
to the top of Jasmine's flowery arch. His
clothes were shimmering gold, perfectly
accessorized with a leaf-green mantle and
slippers. On his head sat a shining crown of
yellow flower stamens. It was Kingcup – the
king of the Flower Fairies.

'Your Majesty . . .' said Jasmine, gazing
in awe at the handsome fairy. Then she

remembered her manners and bobbed a
quick curtsey. 'How can I help you?'

'My dear, you've helped me already . . .
by helping these young fairies,' said the
king. 'We returned from the Fairy Fair some
time ago – to make sure that nobody was
frightened by the shooting stars – and we
didn't want to interrupt your fascinating
talk. We've been eavesdropping, I'm afraid.'

He smiled mischievously. 'I do hope you'll forgive us.'

Us? Jasmine peered over the edge of the flower-woven trellis and gasped. There, far below, was a huge crowd of Flower Fairies. When they spotted her face, they began to clap and cheer.

'Bravo!'

'Fascinating stuff, Jasmine!'

'Loved the bit about the Northern Lights!'

Feeling rather awed at the size of the audience she'd unwittingly entertained, she waved back and then turned to her royal visitor. 'It's only stars and stuff,' she said shyly. 'I watch them every night, you see.'

Kingcup gave a throaty chuckle. 'And to think that *no one* knew you had such an extraordinary hobby . . .' he said, shaking his head. 'I'm so glad we found out. You must dazzle us with your star facts whenever you like, Jasmine.'

'I will,' said Jasmine. 'I promise.' And
with a delighted shiver, she remembered her
daydream in which Flower Fairies gathered
round, eager to hear what she had to say.

The daydream had come true.

Chapter Six
Starry Dreams

There wasn't much time. As Jasmine fluttered down to the ground, she saw that the horizon was glowing faintly and the sky was already losing its deep indigo colour. Soon, the pinpricks of starlight would be snuffed out, like the candles on a birthday cake.

Everyone was sleeping now – everyone except Jasmine. She had a plan. The younger Flower Fairies had been whisked off to their own beds, mumbling sleepily about suns and other worlds and – in Herb Robert's case – swamps and exploding stars. Kingcup had made the most impressive departure, swooping away on the back of a tawny owl.

Now, Jasmine retraced her steps through the garden, moving quickly and quietly to avoid disturbing sleeping fairies. She passed the tall purple foxglove and giggled. Foxglove was still fast asleep, still snoring.

The yellowy-green tent glowed eerily in the fading moonlight. There wasn't a sound coming from within. The children must be fast asleep now – she hoped. Treading softly, Jasmine approached the entrance and peeped inside. Sure enough, the four children were nestled deep inside their sleeping bags, the star chart still clutched tightly in Rahul's hand.

'Boo!'

Even though the voice was barely above

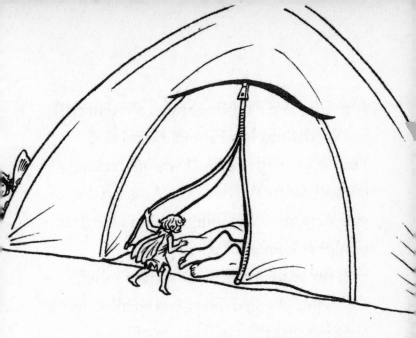

a whisper, Jasmine rocketed upwards
with fright, colliding with the tent and
trampolining helplessly into the air. As she
plummeted back down, her eyes flicked to
and fro. Who *was* it? Was someone spying
on her?

'I say,' said a familiar figure, stepping from
behind the tent. He smiled apologetically. 'I
didn't mean to scare you like that. Terribly
sorry.'

'Dandelion!' hissed Jasmine. 'What are

you *doing* here? I thought you were an elf!'

'No, definitely a Flower Fairy,' said Dandelion with a grin. 'I was just taking a moonlight stroll,' he said. 'Wondered what you were up to, creeping about in the dead of night. Thought I'd say hello!'

Jasmine heaved a great sigh of relief.

'Hello,' she said. She glanced all around, noticing that the sky had grown even paler. She didn't have long. 'Look, there's something I need to do,' she said. 'Can you keep a secret?'

'Absolutely,' said Dandelion, his yellow and black wings twitching with excitement. 'Fire away.'

'Well, what I want to do is this . . .' whispered Jasmine. She leaned closer to the Flower

Fairy's ear and spoke softly.

Dandelion nodded. 'Right-oh. Uh-huh. Yep, got it. Good plan.' He peeked into the tent at the sleeping children and grinned. 'I'll be over there, keeping a lookout,' he whispered. 'Now, hurry. The sun will be up any moment and those larks make an awful racket when they get going.' He scooted over to the foxglove and gave her the thumbs-up.

Jasmine delved her hand into the secret pocket one last time. She'd had such a busy night that the fairy dust was nearly gone, but she scrabbled around and eventually found a few grains nestling at the very bottom of her pocket. Good. That was all she needed. She pinched her fingertips tightly together and lifted them into the air. Then, with one great puff of air, she blew the fairy dust into the tent. For a few seconds it hung shimmering and sparkling in the air – before settling gently on to the sleeping children.

Quietly, she sang:

'Star light, star bright,
The first star I see tonight,
I wish I may, I wish I might
Have the wish I wish tonight ...'

'There, that should do it,' she whispered. The children's dreams would now be filled with stars. 'Thank you!' she whispered to them. 'Thank you *so* much for teaching me all about something so wonderful!' Then she shook Dandelion's hand gratefully before hurrying away.

As the dawn chorus began, the Flower Fairy lay her sleepy head on a pillow of

fragrant blossom. It was morning. But even
though the twinkling stars had faded from
the sky with the rising sun, the starry Jasmine
flowers glimmered all around her still.

The starry night had become a starry day.

Would you like to know which
Flower Fairy you are?

Learn more about your favourite
Flower Fairy friends?

Or find out how to create your
own Flower Fairies Tea Party?

Explore the special 'Secret Stories' area at

www.flowerfairies.com

Featuring

* Exclusive profiles on all the
  fairies in the series

* A sneaky peek inside each book

* Print out and colour favourite
  flower fairy scenes

* Secret Fairy Finder

* Magical Recipes

* Secret Wordsearch

* Special Offers

Don't forget to sign up
for the enchanting Flower Fairies
Newsletter

FLOWER
FAIRIES
FRIENDS

Fairy Fun   Magical Secrets

Secret Stories

Adventure   Fabulous Friendships

Fairy Wishes   Mischief

Did you know that
Lavender has a very
unusual hobby?

That **Strawberry's**
best friend in the world
is Blackberry?

Or that **Candytuft's**
favourite thing to do is making
delicious sweets?

You can find out by reading all **12** exciting fairy-tale
adventures in this gorgeous series and discover the enchanting
world of the Flower Fairies.

FLOWER
FAIRIES

FLO
FAI
FRIE